D0340419

PUPPY
TROUBLE

By Marcia Thornton Jones and Debbie Dadey

Illustrated by Amy Wummer

Hyperion Books for Children
New York

To the original Jack, my neighbor Jack Marvel,
and his family, Abby, Andrea, and Jeff—DD

In memory of the real Tazz and her sister
Purrl!—MTJ

Text copyright © 2001 by Marcia Thornton Jones and Debbie Dadey
Illustrations copyright © 2001 Amy Wummer

Barkley's School for Dogs, Volo, and the Volo colophon are trademarks of
Disney Enterprises, Inc.

Printed in the United States of America
First Edition
1 3 5 7 9 10 8 6 4 2
This book is set in 14-pt. Cheltenham.
ISBN 0-7868-1548-8
Visit www.volobooks.com

Contents

1. Noisy Mutt   1

2. Attack of the Killer Bumblebees   10

3. Sweet Like Cotton Candy   16

4. Scaredy-Mutts   24

5. Puppy Chow   32

6. Wonder Dog   38

7. A Job to Do   45

8. Puppy Tracking   51

9. Too Late   57

10. Puppies to the Rescue   66

NOISY MUTT

"What's up, Fido?" Tazz purred from the arms of her human, Miss Frimple. My human, Maggie, and I stood on the sidewalk outside our apartment building.

"My name is Jack," I growled. Actually, I liked to think of myself as Jack, the Wonder Dog.

This wasn't the first time I'd met up with Tazz. In fact, I had saved that cat's furry tail not too long ago.

"Your dog is frightening my poor Razzmatazz," Miss Frimple said.

"Hush, Jack," Maggie told me, tugging at my leash.

Maybe I was a little grouchy; after all, I'd planned on lying on the couch all day long and taking it easy. Maggie had another idea.

"Come on, Jack," Maggie said sweetly. "It's time for school."

School wasn't all bad, but I sure do like sleeping on the big, soft couch all day—especially when no one is home to tell me to get down on the floor.

"Humph," Miss Frimple snapped, interrupting my thoughts. "This apartment building would be a better place if no dogs were allowed. Why don't you get rid of that noisy mutt and get a nice, quiet cat?"

It's not in my nature to growl at people, but I wanted to growl at Miss Frimple. I didn't get a chance, since Maggie pulled me down the sidewalk.

3

"See you later, chump," Tazz called after us. "And that's a promise."

You could call Tazz bossy. But one thing I knew for sure, you could not call Tazz a liar. If she promised to see me later, I knew it would happen.

Maggie and I walked around the corner of our block to Barkley's School. From the outside it looked like any normal building in our neighborhood with a glass door. Only Barkley's had a small waiting room, a kibble room, and a big play yard filled with tunnels, ladders, and teeter-totters.

I don't really like the good-bye part of the morning. I know Maggie goes to school, too. But I miss her. I wish we could both stay home and play. Plus, who will protect our apartment without me around to bark at strangers?

Fred Barkley, the boss and owner of Barkley's, zipped me out the back door as though he had better things to do. I

barked, just to show him I didn't appreci-
ate the brush-off. Usually, barking gets
Fred upset, but not today. Obviously, he
had other things on his mind.

I'm not bragging when I say that I have
the loudest bark in the entire city. It
starts as a deep rumble in my chest,
works its way up through my throat, and
erupts like a bass drum from my mouth.

My bark has been known to stop traffic, make little old ladies jump, and cause toddlers to clap with joy. That's how good my bark is, and I wanted to use my absolute best bark for the two dogs that were nosing their way toward me. These weren't just any dogs. These were my friends, and they deserved the best.

Blondie pranced right up to me and touched my nose. "Good to see you again," she said in that soft voice of hers.

I'm a bit embarrassed to admit my throat closed up and all I got out was a whimper. That's because it is a Fido Fact that Blondie is the prettiest poodle to walk on grass. Her curly white hair reflected the sun like a halo. Blondie and about eighteen other dogs were lounging around the yard, taking advantage of morning recess.

Not Floyd. Floyd dropped a soggy tennis ball with a wet splat right at my paws. He had a habit of carrying something in his mouth all the time. "Fang-tastic to see you again, Jack," Floyd said. "Wanna play?"

I noticed my old buddy Woodrow snuggled in his pile of rags in a corner. "No time to play," Woodrow warned. "Today is *the* day. Better rest up if you know what's good for you."

"What do you mean, *the* day?" I asked.

Woodrow didn't answer. He couldn't. Sweetcakes came prancing through the

door, and right behind was her drooling pal, Clyde. Sweetcakes was a Doberman pinscher about the size of a truck. She liked to think she was the ruler of the Barkley's School playground. Most dogs were glad to let her believe it. After all, the fact that she was missing part of an ear was poochie proof that Sweetcakes was one dog who didn't run from a fight. Sweetcakes looked straight at me and sniffed the air.

"I thought I smelled something rotten," Sweetcakes said.

"Yeah," the bulldog panted. "Rotten."

I didn't have time to give Clyde and Sweetcakes the growl they deserved because Fred stepped outside. Sweet-cakes licked Fred's hand. "How's my little sweetie-cakes?" Fred asked, scratching his dog's good ear.

I couldn't stand to watch Sweetcakes pretending to be sweet. I spied a bright sunbeam toward the back of the yard and trotted over. I turned three times, like all good dogs do, flopped to the ground, and closed my eyes. I needed a nice long nap.

Too bad I didn't get to sleep very long.

ATTACK OF THE KiLLER BUMBLEBEES

Ouch! It felt like a ten-pound bumblebee attacked my nose. I opened one eye. What was going on?

Ouch! Something bit my tail. Ow! My rump! I yelped and jumped up, both eyes open. Five brown and black puppies took a running leap and landed on my head. It took all my strength to shake them loose. They rolled onto the ground, their fat little bellies up toward the sky. "Cut that out," I told the pups.

I've never heard so much yapping in all

my life. How could something so small make so much noise? Still, I had to admit they were cute. I might not have any pups of my own, but I do have a soft spot for the little critters. Maybe I could take these little guys under my paw and teach them the ways of the Wonder Dog. It made me feel kind of warm and cuddly inside.

Bam! Bam! Puppies began dropping on my body like fleas on a hot summer's day.

Bam! One landed on my back and grabbed on with tiny puppy teeth. "Get off me!" I barked. It didn't do any good, though; the puppy hung on tight and started giggling.

This was not funny. Then I heard Blondie. "Charge!" Blondie yelled. Good friends are like a dog's tail—always there when you need them. I looked up and saw my friends.

Blondie, Floyd, and even Woodrow

came around the doghouse in a blaze of glory. Blondie led the way. She sent puppies flying right and left with her nose. Floyd threw his tennis ball far away from the doghouse. Four puppies flew off me and chased after it. The puppies looked back at us. I could tell they were planning another attack.

Woodrow, who likes to nap more than anything, surprised us all by growling. I didn't even know the old basset hound

had it in him, but it was one heck of a growl. Five of the puppies scattered. I couldn't blame them. Woodrow's growling was enough to give even me nightmares.

One of the puppies didn't look startled. He walked right up to Woodrow and growled back. "You don't scare me, Gramps," the puppy said. "My name is Bubba, and nothing scares me."

Woodrow backed away from the puppy. The puppy followed him and growled again. We were speechless. Even me. And it takes a lot to make me speechless.

"Now, that's my kind of dog," Sweetcakes said. We had been so busy fending off the attack of the killer puppies that none of us noticed Sweetcakes and Clyde sneaking up to watch.

"Yeah, yeah," Clyde said, "our kind of dog."

Sweetcakes took a giant step toward

Bubba and said, "Come with me kid, and I'll teach you a few tricks of my own." Bubba gave us one last look and ran over to Sweetcakes.

"Oh, no," Blondie said. "That's the last thing we need—a Sweetcakes-in-training!"

SWEET LIKE COTTON CANDY

"Where did those puppies come from?" I panted.

"I warned you," Woodrow said. "This is *the* day."

"You keep saying that," I said. "But you won't tell me what you mean."

"Every year Fred gets a new litter of puppies to train," Floyd explained. "Today is puppy day."

I was going to ask more questions, but Fred walked through the back door.

"It's time for lessons," Fred announced.

He had a big bag full of treats in his left hand. When I saw that, all I could think of was treats.

Floyd had the same idea. "Treats, treats," he panted. Dogs appeared from all over the yard. A brown terrier with a bald spot popped out of a tunnel and nosed in front of a tiny Chihuahua.

"Come on, Sweetcakes," Fred called. "Let's show these new little fellows how to behave."

I stared at Fred. I had to wonder if Fred had lost his mind for good.

"How can he call Sweetcakes well-behaved?" I asked Woodrow. "After all, she bullies every dog here."

Woodrow sat down to scratch a flea before answering. "Sweetcakes is more than mean," he finally said. "She's smart, too. She has Fred fooled. He thinks she is sweeter than cotton candy."

"Just watch Sweetcakes," Blondie said.

Fred snapped his fingers and pointed to the tunnel. Sweetcakes dashed through the tunnel, then soared over the bars in the center of the yard. The puppies cheered. A few even tried to follow her.

Next, Fred pointed to the teeter-totter. Sweetcakes headed up the teeter-totter, waited in the middle while it evened out under her weight, then slowly made her way down the other side. She even remembered to step on the yellow edge at the bottom. A dog gets extra points for that. Another puppy followed her, but as soon as Sweetcakes hopped off, the puppy flew into the air. "Wheeeee!" the puppy yelled. Fred was quick. He caught the little guy midair.

As soon as Sweetcakes jumped over a few more bars, she trotted over to Fred and licked his hand. Fred grinned so big, I saw all of his dull teeth. He scratched

Sweetcakes on her one good ear. "You are perfect," Fred said. "You'll be a sure winner in the next dog show."

The whole thing turned my stomach. It made me want to beat Sweetcakes at everything, but one look at that teetertotter made me shake my head.

After Sweetcakes was finished, Fred tried to get all of us to do the same tricks. Let me tell you, those things are harder than they look. Avoiding Sweetcakes and Clyde made them even harder. As soon as Fred looked away, they would growl or yip or make faces, enough to distract any dog.

When the Irish setters tried to jump over the bar, Sweetcakes's low growl made them smack right into the bar with a bang. When the white Westie tried to run through a tunnel, Sweetcakes tripped the little dog. Practically every dog was on the receiving end of one of Sweetcakes's or

Clyde's rotten tricks. The duo didn't bother Woodrow, but they barked at Blondie, causing her to trip on a ladder. That got my blood fighting mad!

It happened to me, too. Fred pushed me onto the teeter-totter. Believe you me, it wasn't my idea. I gave it a good try until that little pup Bubba sneered at me. It startled me, and I'm ashamed to admit I fell right off the edge. I landed on my tail and hurt my pride. I knew Sweetcakes and Clyde had put Bubba up to it. They howled with laughter.

I sank to the ground beside my old basset buddy, Woodrow. Blondie and Floyd dropped down beside us.

Before I closed my eyes for a rest, I saw Sweetcakes and Bubba trot off together. I guess you could call Sweetcakes dependable. You could always depend on her to cause trouble. Whatever she was planning with Bubba was bound to be trouble for the rest of the dogs at Barkley's.

Woodrow must have been thinking the same thing.

"Don't worry," Woodrow told me, settling his nose down on his paws. "Sweetcakes won't have Bubba for long. Fred will see to that."

Blondie nodded her slender white nose. "It happens every year. The pups drive us all crazy for a while. But after Fred trains them, he finds a new family for each one."

"You mean every puppy gets adopted?" I asked.

Floyd rolled his ball around between his paws. "Every last one," he said. "Then it's back to normal here."

It made me a little sad to think about Bubba leaving; after all, the pup had spunk. But it was good to know Bubba and the other puppies would have good homes. In the meantime, how much trouble could Bubba and Sweetcakes cause?

4

SCAREDY-MUTTS

"What a sorry sight," a voice above us purred. Tazz sat on top of the wall, her tail swishing lazily back and forth.

Every dog at Barkley's School knew Tazz. She had a habit of showing up at the absolute worst times.

"How did you get away from Miss Frimple?" I sighed.

"A cat has her ways," Tazz said, stretching her paws.

Woodrow opened his eyes. "How long have you been up there?" he asked.

"Long enough," Tazz said with a yawn. "I saw a group of scaredy-mutts get whipped by puppies."

Tazz wasn't bad—for a cat. But she did have a way of rubbing a dog's hair the wrong way.

"We can handle puppies," Blondie told Tazz. "And we can handle cats, too. So you'd better watch out."

"I'm purr-fectly sure you're right," Tazz said with a twitch of her whiskers. "But can you prove it?" Tazz nodded toward the center of the playground.

Bubba was making his way across the yard, straight toward us. Sweetcakes and Clyde watched from a distance. Clyde giggled until Sweetcakes silenced him with a nip on the nose. "Remember what I told you," Sweetcakes called after Bubba.

Bubba trotted right up to Floyd and sat down. That puppy did not blink an eye. I hate to admit it, but I couldn't help but admire the little tyke, and that means a lot coming from Jack, the Wonder Dog. After all, it does take courage to face down a group of grown-up hounds. That's exactly what Bubba did.

Bubba locked eyes with Floyd. There's nothing a dog hates worse than to be stared at, but Floyd was brave. He stared right back. I figured the puppy would be the first to look away. I was wrong. Floyd gnawed at his tennis ball. Floyd growled.

He even took a step toward Bubba. Floyd wouldn't hurt a flea, and Bubba knew it. The pup didn't budge. Finally, Floyd blinked.

"Want to play?" Floyd asked. That was just like Floyd. Fetching solved every-thing. His solution was if you can't beat them, make them your friend. It was a stroke of genius. Only, because Floyd had the ball in his mouth, it sounded like "Vanta paybe?"

Bubba obviously couldn't understand

mouth-full-of-ball talk, because he didn't smile. He growled.

I heard Clyde laughing out loud. Bubba hadn't budged the entire time. I knew if we didn't do something soon, Bubba would declare himself the winner. Floyd tried to walk away. Bubba followed him, staring the entire time.

The rest of us watched. I didn't know what Floyd would do.

"Let's face it. There's nothing we can do," Woodrow said. "I've been around for

a long time and I've never figured out a way to fight a puppy—especially a puppy trained by Sweetcakes."

I had newfound respect for Woodrow. Woodrow knew the score, and there was more between those long floppy ears than matted hair.

Floyd tried to be friendly one more time. He rolled the ball toward Bubba. "Want to play?" Floyd asked again.

Bubba didn't miss his chance. He grabbed the ball and ran.

"Hey," Floyd said. "Give me back my ball."

Bubba ran back to Sweetcakes and sat between her monster paws. The pup grinned. "If you want this ball," the pup said, "you'll have to come and get it."

"Yeah, yeah," Clyde repeated with a laugh. "Get it."

Clyde wasn't the only one laughing. Sweetcakes laughed so hard she had to sit down on the grass.

"We're doomed," Blondie said. But we'd forgotten one thing—Tazz.

"Oh, for Pete's sake," Tazz groaned from atop the wall. "Must I do everything?" And then, Tazz did the one thing she never should have done.

PUPPY CHOW

Tazz jumped down inside the walls of Barkley's School.

Every dog ear in the yard perked up. Every nose twitched. Including mine. There is something about a bushy cat tail that makes a dog kick into high gear.

Sweetcakes howled a battle cry. "Get the cat!"

"Yeah. Yeah." Clyde panted. "Cat!"

Immediately, dogs darted from every corner of the yard. Even Woodrow raised his head.

"Run, Tazz!" I howled, but I knew there was no escape. A cat trapped inside Barkley's School was a doggy dinner.

Tazz swished her tail high in the air. The fur on her back stood straight up. She faced Bubba and hissed.

For the first time, Bubba blinked. He whimpered. Never, in his short life, had he come face-to-face with a ten-pound angry cat.

Bubba jumped back, but not fast enough. Tazz swatted Bubba right on the nose. Bubba yelped, more in surprise than with pain. "Catch me if you can," Tazz hissed, the sun glinting off her yellow eyes. Then she hightailed it across the yard.

Dogs flew from every corner. I followed. Don't get the wrong idea. I wasn't really chasing the cat. I just wanted to find out what happened. After all, I had to be there if someone should need the services of a Wonder Dog.

Tazz darted in a tunnel. So did the rest of the dogs. Of course, there wasn't room for that many dogs in the tunnel. Three dogs got stuck. One of them was Clyde— but not Bubba and not Sweetcakes. They jumped over the tunnel and were almost to the other side when Tazz shot out of the tunnel.

Tazz was out of places to run. She

backed herself into a corner under a bush with big pink flowers.

"You're dog meat, cat," Sweetcakes said, snarling so her extra-long teeth glistened with slobber.

"Yeah," Bubba echoed. "Puppy chow."

It looked like Tazz was a goner. She may be a cat, but she was also in trouble. It was up to me to save her. I took a step closer to Sweetcakes and Bubba. "Leave the cat alone," I tried to growl. My throat was dry, and it came out more like a whimper.

"Don't worry about me," Tazz told me. Her eyes glinted bravely in the sun.

Bubba's hindquarters wiggled with anticipation. Just as Bubba pounced, Tazz disappeared under the bush. Bubba scrambled after her. The bush shook as if an earthquake had just hit. Then everything grew quiet. Too quiet.

I nosed my way closer to the bush. So did Sweetcakes. We both sniffed.

"Bubba?" Sweetcakes called.

"Tazz?" I whined.

There was no answer. They had disappeared.

WONDER DOG

Sweetcakes and I scrambled under the bush. There, in the corner of the wall, was a hole the perfect size for a cat and puppy to squeeze through.

"This is all your fault," I told Sweetcakes.

"Hey, I didn't tell that puppy to go through the hole," Sweetcakes argued.

"No," Blondie said as she wiggled under the bush beside me. "But you did try to turn that puppy into a bully. He thought he had to catch the cat just to

please you," Blondie said to Sweet-cakes.

Sweetcakes snarled at Blondie. "Nobody pleases me," Sweetcakes told us.

"Yeah, yeah," Clyde repeated, sticking his nose under the bush. "Nobody."

"Too bad Bubba didn't know you never meant to be his friend," Blondie said.

"Nobody is my friend," Sweetcakes said.

"Nobody?" Clyde asked sadly. He sat

down and looked up at Sweetcakes.

"Nobody," Sweetcakes said again.

Sweetcakes usually made my blood boil, but for once I wasn't mad at her. I was sad, instead. Blondie must have thought the same thing. "That is nothing to brag about," she said softly.

Just then, Fred came out the back door. Sweetcakes glared at all of us. "I don't need any of you," she said. "I have Fred on my side." Then she backed out from under the bush and pranced away to Fred's side. She wasn't the only one. Four puppies frolicked over Fred's shoes.

Fred scratched Sweetcakes's ears. "You're such a good dog," Fred cooed. "Have you been taking care of our little puppies?"

"How can Fred believe Sweetcakes is a good dog?" I asked.

Suddenly, Fred let out a howl of his own. "Where is Bubba?" he yelled. "He can't be gone! I have plans for him. He's my new prizewinner!"

"Uh-oh," Woodrow said. "It looks like Sweetcakes just lost her one and only friend."

"Hey," Sweetcakes yipped. "I'm your prizewinner. You don't need that puppy! You still have me!" Fred didn't answer, since he couldn't understand dog talk.

"Do you think that rotten Sweetcakes knew about this the entire time?" Blondie asked.

"She is one monster of a dog," Floyd said with a nod. "If she knew Fred planned to keep Bubba, it would be just like her to trick Bubba into getting into trouble."

"Poor Bubba," Woodrow said, his eyes looking sadder than ever. "He trusted Sweetcakes."

"Bubba!" Fred yelled. "Where are you, Bubba?"

"I bet we don't get our kibble on time," Floyd mumbled.

I sighed and plopped down on the ground. I felt bad. I'll even admit I felt a little guilty. After all, we knew Sweetcakes could never be trusted. We should have warned Bubba.

Floyd dropped his ball right in front of my nose. "We have to find the puppy," Floyd said. "If we don't, Fred will put us all in time-out while he searches for him."

"This is worse than an afternoon in

time-out," Blondie pointed out. "Bubba knows nothing of the outside world."

"Blondie is right," Woodrow said with a wise nod. "Cars. Strangers. Kids with sticky fingers. Bubba doesn't know about those kinds of dangers. He'll never survive."

I sat up straight. "Yes, he will. Because we're going to save him."

"There's no way out of here," Blondie said. "We're too big to fit through that hole."

I looked around the yard. Suddenly, I knew what to do. After all, rescuing puppies was a job for a Wonder Dog. "If we're too big to go under the wall," I said slowly, "then we'll have to go over it."

Woodrow looked up at the wall. "There is no way these short legs can get over that tall wall," he said.

"Don't worry," I told my pals. "I have an idea!"

7

A JOB TO DO

"It's too dangerous," Blondie said after I explained my plan.

"It will never work," Woodrow added.

Floyd didn't say a word. He didn't have to. I could tell Floyd didn't like the idea by the way he gnawed on his tennis ball.

"We have no choice," I nearly growled. "But I can't do it alone. Can I count on you for help?"

Blondie looked at Woodrow. The concern in her big brown eyes nearly broke my heart. Woodrow's face wrinkled with even more lines. They both looked at Floyd. Floyd dropped his ball. "You can always count on us," Floyd said.

Woodrow nodded. "We're friends to the end."

I led the way to the teeter-totter. As I perched on one end, Blondie reached out her delicate paw and placed it gently on mine. "Are you sure you want to try this?" she asked.

I straightened my body and nodded. I

tried not to let her see my hind legs trembling. "Let's do it," I said. I swallowed once while Woodrow counted to three. Then, with a flying leap, all three of my friends jumped onto the high end of the teeter-totter.

My end flew up, and I went up with it. I used my powerful back legs to spring even higher in the air. I heard the cheers of my friends as I sailed up, up, and up over the top of the wall to freedom.

Flying isn't as easy it looks. Landing is even harder. The ground knocked every last breath of air from my lungs and stars twinkled in front of my eyes.

When I finally gulped in enough air to make all the stars disappear, I stood up and took in my surroundings. Barkley's School backed right up to my favorite place of all time. The park. The sight of all those trees made me forget about Bubba and Tazz.

I yipped. I barked. I was ready to take off running when something landed right on top of me and knocked me back to the ground. "Oops! Sorry about that," Blondie said as she scrambled away.

"What are you doing here?" I asked.

Blondie blinked her big brown eyes at me. "I couldn't let you face danger on your own," she said.

Her words made my heart thump extra hard, and I grinned. "Thanks," I said.

"Come on, we don't have much time," Blondie interrupted. "Bubba could be in serious danger." Blondie didn't wait for me to answer. She trotted off, her nose to the ground.

I sighed. The trees would have to wait for later. Right now, Jack the Wonder Dog had a job to do.

8

PUPPY TRACKING

With my Wonder Dog nose to the ground, I zigzagged through the park. Tracking Bubba was easy. I smelled the same smell I had smelled the minute I had stepped into Barkley's School that morning. Puppy smell.

Blondie followed, with her eyes wide. It's a good thing she watched. A dog gets sort of distracted when he's tracking. "Watch out!" Blondie yelped.

I jumped out of the way just as a kid on roller skates zoomed by. "Be more careful, Jack," Blondie said.

I nodded, then picked up the puppy scent again.

"Oh, no," Blondie whined. "It looks like they left the park." We had reached a road. Cars swished by so fast they could make a dog downright confused. I know that for a fact because I definitely felt a little sick to my stomach.

"Will we have to cross the street?" Blondie asked with a whimper.

I sniffed the sidewalk. The smell of cat and puppy was mixed in with at least three thousand other smells. I turned one way, then another. I turned so many times I got dizzy and had to sit down for three good scratches. I hated to admit it, but I had lost the trail.

Just then, a familiar voice came from the tree branches above. "It's about time you got here," Tazz said. "I thought I'd go crazy keeping my eye on that foolish Bubba."

That voice could only belong to one beast. I looked up at the branches hanging over the sidewalk. Sure enough, Tazz's bushy tail swept from side to side.

"Get down from there and help us find the puppy," I barked at Tazz.

Tazz sighed. "Must I do *everything*?" she asked. "Very well."

Without waiting for an answer, the cat let out a yowl that set the hair on my neck standing straight up. A bicycle rider screeched to a halt. A woman in high heels teetered over and fell. Two kids playing with a ball stopped and pointed to the tree. They weren't the only ones that heard Tazz.

Bubba came tearing through the park. Tazz patiently waited until Bubba was almost to the tree. Then she flew out of the branches and tore down the sidewalk.

Bubba didn't even recognize us. All

that puppy saw was Tazz's tail. Bubba dodged Blondie and went right between my legs. There was nothing left for us to do. We had to follow.

I sped past people, skirted around a messenger on a bicycle, and sailed over a bench. People yelled and hollered, and let me tell you, some of the words weren't exactly nice. But I didn't slow down.

I knew these sidewalks. So did Tazz. They led straight back to our apartment.

My building was in sight. Tazz scampered up the steps just as the front door opened.

The one and only Miss Frimple stepped out of the building. "Here, Tazz," she yelled in a voice that reminded me of tires screeching on cement.

Tazz darted between Miss Frimple's legs. Bubba didn't pay any attention to Miss Frimple. He had one goal in mind. *Get the cat!*

Blondie was close on Bubba's tail. I had to stop them before it was too late. It was Jack, the Wonder Dog to the rescue. Unfortunately, I wasn't fast enough.

TOO LATE

Miss Frimple landed on the sidewalk in a tangle of dogs. Tazz leaped to safety and perched on a window ledge.

I tried to pull Blondie and Bubba away. Instead of grabbing puppy hair, I ended up with a mouthful of Miss Frimple's dress. I heard the fabric tear. I knew that couldn't be good.

Miss Frimple grabbed Blondie and me by the collars. "I have had it with you and your friends," Miss Frimple said so loudly it made my supersensitive ears ache.

I had to let her know that I was only try-ing to help. I barked, extra loud so she'd be sure to hear.

"Don't you sass me," Miss Frimple said.

I glanced up at Tazz and whimpered. "How about a little help?" I asked.

Tazz calmly used a paw to wipe an ear clean. "I'm afraid I've helped enough for one day," she said as she stretched and yawned. "That little dash through the park ruffled my fur. Besides, it's time for my afternoon catnap."

It's not in my nature to beg a cat for help. I'm a dog, after all. But right then I would have pleaded with a hundred cats for help.

I didn't, of course, because Miss Frimple dragged Blondie and me the entire two blocks to Barkley's School for Dogs. Bubba didn't know what else to do, so he followed.

Miss Frimple threw open the door to Barkley's School and pulled us all the way to the backyard. Fred was there, still searching for the missing puppy.

I must admit, it hurt me all the way down to my paws that Fred hadn't even noticed Blondie and I were missing.

Woodrow and Floyd greeted us with delighted yelps.

Sweetcakes looked down her nose at us. "You're back," she said with a growl. "What a pity."

"Yeah, yeah," Clyde panted. "Pity."

Bubba's tail wagged as soon as he saw Sweetcakes. "Aren't you happy to see me?" Bubba asked.

"Hhhhmmm," Sweetcakes said as she looked down her pointy nose at the pup. "About as glad as seeing a troop of ticks."

Bubba's tail stopped wagging and got downright droopy.

Fred, on the other hand, grinned at Bubba. "I'm so glad you found my new prizewinning puppy," he told Miss Frimple. "I was worried sick."

"You should worry," Miss Frimple told Fred. "These beasts of yours were terrorizing the neighborhood. Wait until the police hear how they attacked my poor innocent cat. Then they came after me."

Of course, that was not how it happened at all. Miss Frimple had it all wrong. I barked several times to let Fred know Miss Frimple was not telling the dog-honest truth, especially the part about Tazz being innocent.

"Hush, Jack," Fred said.

Sweetcakes snickered at me. Then she did something so dog-awful it surprised even me. She pushed Bubba right between Miss Frimple's two feet.

Miss Frimple glared down at Bubba. "It's bad enough that you keep a yard full of dogs," Miss Frimple said. "But that puppy is a menace to us all. Did you see how he just tried to trip me?" Miss Frimple pointed right at Bubba.

The little guy backed up and bumped into my front legs. He started to shake and leaned against me. "That . . . that . . . that was mean," Bubba whimpered.

I sighed. I knew what I had to do. I had to get Miss Frimple away from Bubba. Fast. There was only one answer to this puppy problem.

Faster than a flea can jump, I grabbed the first thing I saw—Miss Frimple's purse. I ran as quickly as my Wonder Dog legs could go, which is pretty speedy, if I do say so myself.

"My handbag!" Miss Frimple screamed. "That dog stole my bag. Get him!"

Every dog in the yard heard her cry, especially the puppies. They saw her purse dangling from my jaws of steel and sprang into action. Puppies came at me from every direction. When two skidded under my belly, I tumbled. Another puppy clamped onto my tail. A fourth little guy

grabbed my ear. I did the only thing possible.

I dropped that purse and ran. The puppies latched onto Miss Frimple's purse and tugged. Unfortunately, they pulled in different directions. I knew that by the time those puppies got through with Miss Frimple's purse, there wouldn't be a strap left to floss her teeth with.

"As soon as I get my hands on those mutts, they're going to the pound," Miss Frimple screamed.

The older dogs scattered as she stomped across the yard. Not the puppies. They were too busy playing tug-of-war with her handbag to notice.

Surely, things couldn't get any worse, could they?

10

PUPPIES TO THE RESCUE

Miss Frimple grabbed her purse just as Fred caught me. "That's it!" Fred snapped. "You're going to time-out."

Fred apologized to Miss Frimple before dragging me around a shed and hooking me up to the brick wall. I was almost glad to be leaving the constant stream of meanness coming from Miss Frimple's mouth.

Blondie, Woodrow, and Floyd waited until Fred had left to sneak around the building to see me. "I'm sorry you're in trouble," Floyd said. "Here, you can have my tennis ball." I looked down at Floyd's tattered ball. The entire thing was covered with slobber. Still, Floyd was a good friend. I accepted his gift.

Blondie wasn't so nice. "Have you lost your mind?" she asked. "Miss Frimple will never forgive you."

I sighed and plopped down on the ground. I knew I'd done a crazy thing. Miss Frimple would tell Maggie. Maggie

would have to get rid of me now for sure. I couldn't explain it myself. I was feeling about as low as a dog could get. "Things can't get any worse," I whimpered.

Of course, Sweetcakes proved me wrong when she trotted up. "With you chained to that wall, you'll be out of my way. I'll take care of that troublesome puppy once and for all."

Sweetcakes didn't count on one thing. Puppy power!

A whole gang of puppies roared around the corner with Bubba in the lead. The puppies tumbled to a stop right in front of Sweetcakes.

"Leave Jack alone," Bubba said. "You're nothing but a big bully."

Nobody, and I mean nobody, talked to Sweetcakes that way. It was a Fido Fact, but Bubba didn't care.

Sweetcakes growled and took a giant step toward Bubba. "Watch your step."

Bubba didn't budge. Instead, he locked his big brown eyes and stared at Sweetcakes. Things were going from bad to worse quicker than it takes to gobble a doggy treat.

"You don't really want to hurt Bubba," I told Sweetcakes.

"That's right," Blondie said. "Think of Fred. He's got big plans for Bubba."

Woodrow nodded. "And his plans won't include you if he catches you chewing up Bubba."

Sweetcakes paused for a minute. A hurt look flashed across her face. For a tail-wagging second I almost felt sorry for her. After all, she had thought Fred was her one and only friend.

The second passed. Sweetcakes grinned wickedly. "No problem. Fred will think Jack did it. After all, he's the mutt who always ends up in time-out."

"We have to stop Sweetcakes," Floyd said.

I strained my chain, but there was no way to save Bubba in time. "Run," I howled. "Before it's too late."

Bubba didn't budge. Instead, he called back to his puppy pals. "To the garbage cans!" he yelped. Before Sweetcakes could pounce on Bubba, puppies flew off the trash cans onto Sweetcakes. She looked like a crazy Christmas tree with big puppy ornaments dangling from all over her. Puppies hung from her tail, her ears, and her back.

Sweetcakes shook with all her might, but those puppy teeth hung on tight. I didn't know how long those puppies could hold on, but it was long enough. Sweetcakes finally yelped, "I give up! "Get them off me!"

"Back off," Bubba said with a crooked grin. The puppies jumped off Sweetcakes and hightailed it around the building. Only Bubba stayed behind.

"Fang-tastic!" Floyd cheered. "That was dog-awesome!"

"You know," I said to Bubba, "you're not such a bad pup after all."

Bubba smiled. "I think I'm going to like this place," he said. I liked the idea that Bubba would be around for a while. I had a feeling a Wonder Dog could learn a lot from a pup like Bubba. And maybe I could teach him a few things, too.

"Don't get too comfy," Sweetcakes said as she sulked away. "Because you haven't seen the last of me, fleabag!"

I sighed. I knew our problems were far from over. But one thing was for sure. With trustworthy friends by my side, Barkley's School wasn't such a bad place after all.

ABOUT THE AUTHORS

Marcia Thornton Jones and Debbie Dadey used to work together at the same elementary school—Marcia taught in the classroom and Debbie was a librarian. But now they love writing about a totally different kind of school . . . where the students have four legs and a tail!

Marcia lives in Lexington, Kentucky, and Debbie lives in Fort Collins, Colorado. Their own pets have inspired them to write about Jack and his friends at *Barkley's School*. These authors have also written *The Adventures of the Bailey School Kids*, *The Bailey City Monsters*, and *Triplet Trouble* together.